Library of Congress Cataloging-in-Publication Data
Flesher, Vivienne.   Alfred's nose / Vivienne Flesher. —1st ed.   p. cm.
Summary: Even though everybody loves him as he is, Alfred, a French bulldog,
finds it hard to accept his unusual looks, especially his nose.
ISBN-13: 978-0-06-084313-7 (trade bdg.)
ISBN-13: 978-0-06-084314-4 (lib. bdg.)
[1. French bulldog—Fiction. 2. Bulldog—Fiction. 3. Nose—Fiction.
4. Self-acceptance—Fiction. 5. Dogs—Fiction.] I. Title.
PZ7.F6274Alf 2008   [E]—dc22   2007006884   CIP   AC

1 2 3 4 5 6 7 8 9 10   ❖   First Edition

ALFRED'S NOSE

Vivienne Flesher

KATHERINE TEGEN BOOKS
An Imprint of HarperCollins*Publishers*

Library of Congress Cataloging-in-Publication Data
Flesher, Vivienne.   Alfred's nose / Vivienne Flesher. —1st ed.   p. cm.
Summary: Even though everybody loves him as he is, Alfred, a French bulldog,
finds it hard to accept his unusual looks, especially his nose.
ISBN-13: 978-0-06-084313-7 (trade bdg.)
ISBN-13: 978-0-06-084314-4 (lib. bdg.)
[1. French bulldog—Fiction. 2. Bulldog—Fiction. 3. Nose—Fiction.
4. Self-acceptance—Fiction. 5. Dogs—Fiction.] I. Title.
PZ7.F6274Alf 2008   [E]—dc22   2007006884   CIP   AC

1 2 3 4 5 6 7 8 9 10   ❖   First Edition

This book is dedicated to Alfred's many friends

Everyone loved Alfred.

He was always ready to play **ball**, he liked toys, and he smelled like **popcorn**.

Most of all, children loved his silly, round face and his big, **sloppy kisses**.

Sadly, Alfred did not like the way he looked. He thought his face was **all wrong**. His head was as round as a pumpkin.

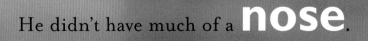

He didn't have much of a **nose**.

And his **tongue** hung out of his mouth. All of the time.

In fact, some children didn't recognize that Alfred was even a dog. Maybe he was a **bat**. Or a **walrus**. Others thought he was sticking his tongue out at them.

And **then** there were the **ants**.

They often took a **shortcut** across Alfred's tongue as he napped.

Alfred's **mother** told him that in some countries ants are considered quite **tasty**.

She also reminded Alfred how much children **adored** his looks. But mothers always think their babies look **beautiful**.

One day Alfred was invited to a dress-up party. He was quite excited because he thought a **costume** was the perfect solution to his problem.

Two girls at the party were dressed as princesses. They suggested that Alfred dress as a **princess** too.

But Alfred didn't think **pink** was his color.

Next he tried a **devil** costume.

It just looked silly.

He tried on a pair of **glasses**,
but he couldn't keep them from
slipping off his flat nose.

He tried on a **coonskin hat**,
but decided he'd rather chew it.

No disguise seemed right.
Then he noticed two boxes of
animal noses.

He **tried** a lovely crocodile snout,
but it frightened even Alfred.

He tried on a duck's bill, but it was
the wrong color.

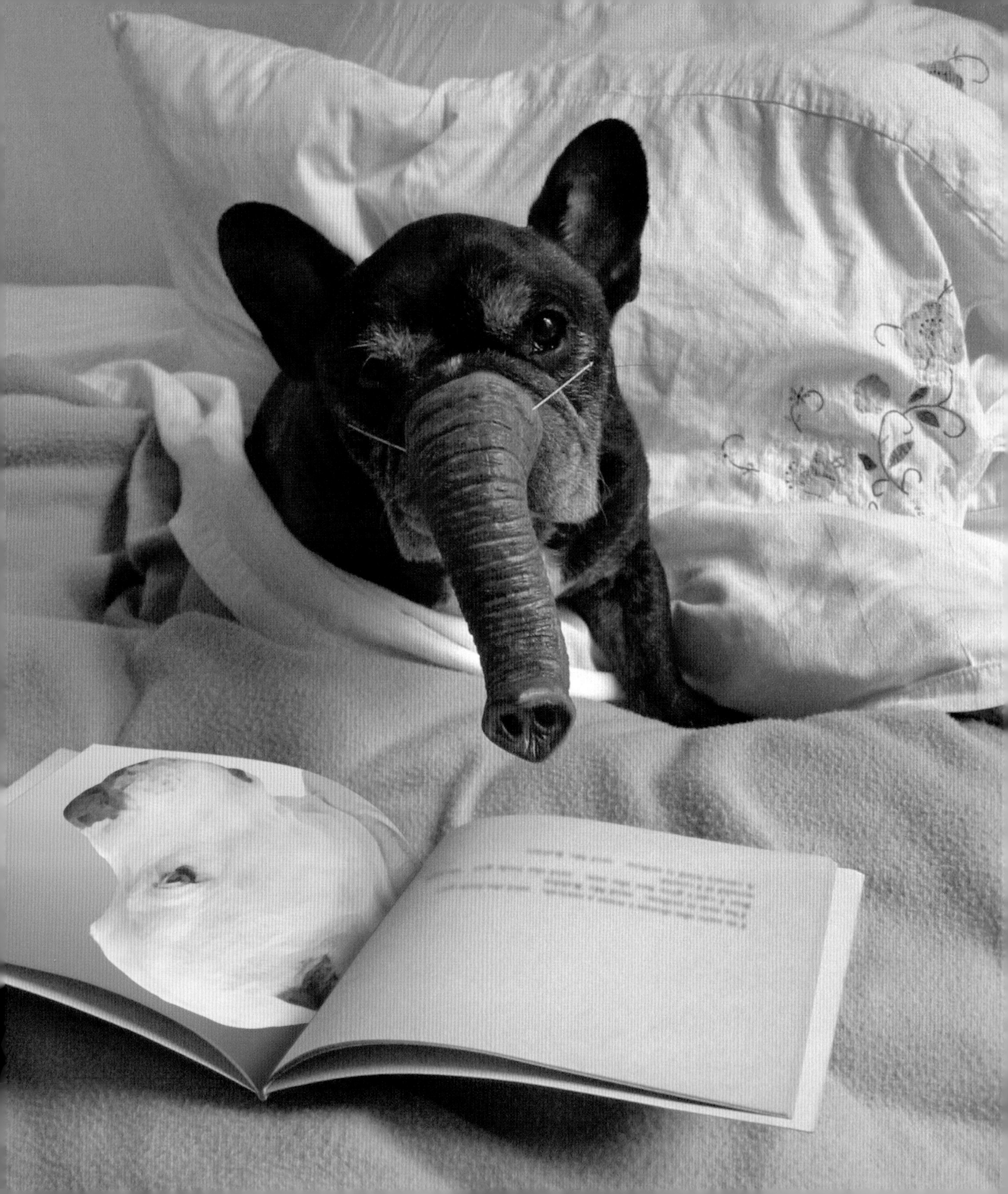

He tried on an **elephant trunk**, but it was so long, Alfred couldn't see the book he was reading.

Finally he tried on a fake dog snout. It looked wonderful! Like a proper dog nose.

"But," one of the girls pointed out, "none of these noses **covers your tongue!"**

So Alfred tried on a **cow's** nose. It covered his tongue completely.

Then Alfred started to worry. How would he eat?

Worse, one of Alfred's friends began to cry. She thought he looked scary. Alfred tried to lick away her **tears**, but the mask got in his way. And what about those sloppy kisses?

Alfred ripped off the mask and everyone cheered.

"We love you just the way you are, Alfred!" they said.

He kissed his friends.

But there was still **one small problem.**

That night, before Alfred even closed his eyes,
the **ants** began crawling across his **tongue**.
So he did what **any dog** would do . . .

Tasty.

Just like his mother had said.